Chekhov's Ladies

Seven Short Tales Adapted for the Stage

by Jules Tasca

Baker's Plays
c/o Samuel French, Inc.
45 West 25th Street
New York, NY 10010
bakersplays.com

MUSIC USE NOTE

Licensees are solely responsible for obtaining formal written permission from copyright owners to use copyrighted music in the performance of this play and are strongly cautioned to do so. If no such permission is obtained by the licensee, then the licensee must use only original music that the licensee owns and controls. Licensees are solely responsible and liable for all music clearances and shall indemnify the copyright owners of the play and their licensing agent, Baker's Plays, against any costs, expenses, losses and liabilities arising from the use of music by licensees.

IMPORTANT BILLING AND CREDIT REQUIREMENTS

All producers of CHEKHOV'S LADIES *must* give credit to the Author of the Play in all programs distributed in connection with performances of the Play, and in all instances in which the title of the Play appears for the purposes of advertising, publicizing or otherwise exploiting the Play and/ or a production. The name of the Author *must* appear on a separate line on which no other name appears, immediately following the title and *must* appear in size of type not less than fifty percent of the size of the title type. Also, the following notice must appear on all printed programs, "Produced by special arrangement with Baker's Plays."

CONTENTS

CHEKHOV'S LADIES can be done as a full evening, or individually as needed. The introduction and Chekhov's commentary can easily be eliminated.

A NOTE ON ADAPTATION

Taking a story that was composed for a single reader and transmuting it into a vehicle for stage presentation is, I've found, not understood by everyone.

To some, the process is simply extracting dialogue from a short story or a novel that someone else has written and having actors use that as a theater piece. I'm sure that in some dialogue driven short stories this can be attempted, but in most – many – cases the story dialogue does not speak, as it should for actors, even though it reads well.

Most narrative work needs to be re-thought and re-designed by the theater artist for stage presentation. The alchemy involved should never be perceived by the audience, that is, the audience need not see the novel or the short story, but should be, in the new group dynamic of actor to audience, witnessing a unique artistic experience, one that a single mind reading cannot.

How much does this change the matrix from which the stage piece emanates? The adaptation should be true to the theme or thought of the original. It should comprise the principal characters, even though composite or even new characters become necessary for dramatic purposes and out of necessity are devised. Most importantly, I believe that the stage adaptation should retain the comic or tragic spirit of the original. Why? Because a stage adaptation is an attempt to share with a live audience a collective (as opposed to the individual) witnessing of the original story told in the present tense.

In adapting Chekhov's stories, I have, perforce, taken certain liberties in architectonics and dialogue, but I have attempted to fully capture the characters and the conflict which the master storyteller envisioned. Also I have retained, I think, the idea in each tale that binds the story and makes it whole.

It is then my hope that these short plays are first cousins to the original short works of Anton Chekhov.

-Jules Tasca

*In memory of Ken Terrell,
one of New York City's finest theater artists.*

CHEKHOV. Good evening, my name is Anton Chekhov. I am happy to see you here tonight to meet some of the women I've written about. I am a medical doctor and a doctor's office in the late 19th century was one of the few places, indeed one of the few sanctuaries, where women of all ages could unburden themselves by telling their physician their deepest concerns. That, coupled with many female acquaintances I made socially, induced me to begin telling their stories. Oh, of course, I've written about men and boys, even dogs, but my female creations have always been more of a fascination to me. The female is a great ocean of mystery whose secrets are never fully uncovered or understood. But please, remember, in my Russia, women were the lower caste in the little hierarchy of Homo Sapiens. Intelligent women suffered by not being taken seriously and those not as intelligent just suffered other deprivation. I remember my own mother being beaten by my father. Yes, my brothers and I were beaten, too, but as men we could run off and set ourselves free… But instead of me chattering on, let us take you out of the modern world tonight and invite you back to Russia…Russia at the turn of the twentieth century…I have played on the stage, myself, so don't be surprised when I take part in some of these plays…Let's start with *The Strange Death of Natasha Probkin.*

THE STRANGE DEATH OF NATASHA PROBKIN
9

CHARACTERS

DOCTOR TREFON KERBELOV - a doctor in his forties

VERANKA - a maid

ALEXY PROBKIN - an aristocrat in his late thirties

SETTING

A bedroom.

TIME

Turn of the Century Russia.

(In the dark we hear a baby cry. The cry fades as lights come up in Natasha Probkin's bedroom. Lamplight. **NATASHA** *lies motionless in her bed. She is covered up to her neck in a blanket.* **VERANKA,** *a maid, stands by the bed weeping. After a beat,* **DOCTOR TREFON KERBELOV** *enters.)*

DOCTOR.. Veranka?…Veranka?…

VERANKA. Oh, Doctor…Oh my…

DOCTOR.. What is it? Why did you send for me to come up? Veranka, stop crying. Where's the baby?

VERANKA. Katenka put him in the other room.

DOCTOR.. Why? So Natasha can sleep? Did Natasha ask to have the boy taken in to the next room? Speak up.

VERANKA.. Mrs. Probkin, she…she…

(The **DOCTOR** *hurries to the bed.)*

DOCTOR. Is there something wrong with her?

(The **DOCTOR** *lightly taps her cheeks. Then he listens to her heart. He hears nothing. He tries smelling salts that he takes from his pocket to no avail.)*

DOCTOR. She's…Veranka, your mistress is dead.

VERANKA. I know that…I sent Katenka to fetch you…I didn't know what to do…

DOCTOR. How did you know she was dead? I don't understand… Stop crying, please. Look, ring for Mr. Probkin to come up…Veranka…

*(***VERANKA*** crosses and pulls a cord on the wall.)*

DOCTOR. The baby is sleeping?

VERANKA. In the other room. Yes…

DOCTOR. Veranka, when I left this room a healthy woman had just given birth and an hour later I find her…

(**ALEXY PROBKIN** *enters with a drink in his hand*)

ALEXY. What's going on? Trefon?

DOCTOR. Alexy, listen...

ALEXY. Why'd you ring for me, Veranka? Why'd you send for the doctor? Veranka?

(**VERANKA** *starts to cry again.*)

ALEXY. Trefon?

DOCTOR. Alexy, I have horrible news.

ALEXY. What news? Where's my son? Is the baby all right?

DOCTOR. Your son's asleep in the adjoining room.

(**ALEXY** *crosses to the bed.*)

ALEXY. Natasha...Natasha...Natasha!

DOCTOR. She's...She's gone. I'm sorry, Alexy.

ALEXY. Gone? How? Jesus, but an hour ago she was...

DOCTOR. I don't know. There were no problems when I left her resting. None. Only an autopsy would show what...

ALEXY. Veranka, you were here with her! Did she give any sign of distress? Did she? Stop crying and answer me!

VERANKA. I'm sorry, Sir.

ALEXY. Why didn't you send for the doctor sooner? Veranka, what happened up here, woman? Tell me. How could she be gone?...Natasha, how could you leave me like this? Natasha, oh God, Natasha...Veranka, I want to know exactly what happened up here. Veranka!

DOCTOR. Alexy, the woman's distraught, too. She was close to Natasha...Veranka, come here and sit...

(**VERANKA** *sits.*)

Look, it's normal for everyone to be upset. Would you like some brandy?

(**VERANKA** *shakes her head no.*)

Are you all right to talk a little?

VERANKA. I'm sorry...I'm all right to talk...I'm all right... Yes...

DOCTOR. I want to ask you some questions, that's all. You understand? Good. Now after the baby had been cleaned up and the sheets changed and all of that, I left Natasha resting. But aside from being tired, she was all right.

VERANKA. She said…She said…She said she was going to die.

DOCTOR. What?

ALEXY. She would say that to me, too.

DOCTOR. She…When, Alexy?

ALEXY. It was some quirk, I thought. Some quirk of pregnant women to say outrageous things. I…I mentioned to her in the summer that I planned to buy two new horses for the carriage and she said to me, "It's nothing to me, Alexy. By summer, my home will be a grave."

VERANKA. She talked that way to me, too, Doctor. "As soon as I give birth, I will be no more," she said, just like that. "I will be no more." She told the cook and the groundskeeper the same thing. Yes, she did.

DOCTOR. I'm baffled. In my judgment Natasha Probkin was young, in good health and of intelligent mind. Why? Why would she just die? Alexy, what did you think when she admitted these black thoughts to you?

ALEXY. I never believe women's premonitions. Any woman's. Not even my mother's gloomy predictions about life. Never. It's just…It's just women's hysterics.

VERANKA. I don't think so, Sir.

ALEXY. Are you contradicting me, Veranka?

VERANKA. I'm saying…I'm just saying…I know…

DOCTOR. Veranka?

VERANKA. I know what happened, Doctor, but the Lord knows I don't want to get into any trouble. No. But I don't like to hear Madame Probkin talked about that way, because I know what happened.

ALEXY. What? What happened? Veranka?

DOCTOR. There'll be no trouble, I promise you, for telling us anything you can…Go on…It's all right…

VERANKA. I was up here today when Madame Probkin... When she...

DOCTOR. It's all right. You'll be in no trouble for just speaking up...

VERANKA. You think not, but Mr. Probkin will let me go... I'll lose my position in this house by saying...

ALEXY. Listen here, woman, I have a dead wife here and you're worrying about your position? Why would you be told to leave?

VERANKA. Doesn't matter. Maybe. Maybe I don't want to stay here anymore...No. After I find a wet nurse for that baby, I...I'd probably go off anyway. So I guess it doesn't matter...

DOCTOR. Veranka, I can get a wet nurse here in half an hour. Stick to the point. What happened to Natasha?

VERANKA. It...It all started a while ago, Doctor. Madame was pregnant with her boy. At that time, we had a guest staying here. One of Madame Probkin's cousins, Vera, her name was.

ALEXY. Natasha told you about that?

VERANKA. She told me the whole thing, yes...Oh, God...

DOCTOR. Alexy, what is it?

ALEXY. Nothing...Nothing...I had a few drinks too many, that's all.

DOCTOR. A few drinks too many? So what? When?

ALEXY. It's nothing, I tell you, Trefon. Believe me...

VERANKA. The cousin came for a weekend visit. Not a smart girl, you know, a head like a bird's nest. That kind.

ALEXY. What has her cousin Vera got to do with her lying dead? Jesus, that was months and months ago!

DOCTOR. What are you trying to say, Veranka?

ALEXY. Oh, tell him and get it over with and he'll see it's nothing.

DOCTOR. This cousin, Vera, what did she do?

VERANKA. Madame woke up in the middle of the night feeling upset, queasy, you know. She said she heard sounds...

DOCTOR. Sounds?

VERANKA. Sounds in the guest room. She told me she went in and she…she found them, Doctor…

ALEXY. I was drunk. It was nothing, I tell you. Nothing at all.

DOCTOR. Natasha said she saw them together in bed?!

(**VERANKA** *shakes her head, "yes." Then she begins to cry.*)

ALEXY. Trefon, it was stupid, I know. A lapse brought on by vodka. I admit it. She – Natasha was pregnant, not feeling like her usual self. She was constantly ill, you know how these things are. That night, I was…yes, I'd gotten tipsy. Vodka does strange things to men. I regretted it in sobriety. It was nothing. Her cousin, God, a beast of a girl. It was nothing. Listen to me, Trefon. I explained it all to Natasha in the morning. I told her that her cousin, Vera, had been drinking with me and…and…

DOCTOR. And you explained that vodka does strange things to women, too.

ALEXY. She accepted it. You know how understanding a woman Natasha was. She said she believed me and that it was water under the bridge. That same morning, Vera left and Natasha never invited her back.

DOCTOR. So…Veranka, I still don't know how this woman died…Veranka…Veranka…what else happened…this evening? What happened?

VERANKA. Madame poisoned herself…

ALEXY. Poisoned herself? She would never…No…She'd never…

DOCTOR. Wait, Alexy…Veranka, how do you know she poisoned herself?

VERANKA. She told me so, Doctor. Right from that bed. I can still hear Madame's voice. She told me…

ALEXY. Told you what?

VERANKA. After she sobbed out the whole story of her cousin. She swallowed it. I didn't know what it was she swallowed…

*(The **DOCTOR** crosses to the night stand and opens a drawer.)*

ALEXY. Why in hell didn't you immediately run downstairs for Doctor Kerbelov?

VERANKA. She'd already taken the poison when she told me, Sir. She asked me to lean over the bed and I did and she said, "I've taken enough to kill me."

DOCTOR. *(holding a bottle)* A powerful derivative of morphine.

ALEXY. Why didn't you send for us, you foolish woman?!

DOCTOR. Alexy, leave her alone! She did send for me. By the time I got up here, she was dead. This is a quick acting drug. I couldn't have reversed the effect.

ALEXY. Why? Why did she do such a thing?

DOCTOR. Obviously, Natasha didn't want to live anymore.

ALEXY. She just had my child! What mother gives birth and then…then…Just…just…

VERANKA. I asked her that, Sir. That very same question.

ALEXY. And she said?…

VERANKA. She said, "Veranka, it is easier to die than to forgive."

ALEXY. Easier to die than to forgive…

VERANKA. That's what she said. Then she held my hand tight and smiled…Then…then…nothing…

ALEXY. It couldn't be that…It couldn't be…No…She told me…She told me…She said…Natasha!

*(**ALEXY** puts his head in his hands and sobs. The **DOCTOR** pulls the blanket over Natasha's face as the lights fade.)*

CHEKHOV. Such a vital life coming to a sad end. The poison now in Alexy is slow acting and it will bring him a more painful end…

My next story, *Vierochka*, observes a young girl's yearnings and how intensely they live in a young heart…

YOUNG VIEROCHKA

17

CHARACTERS

IVAN OGINOV - a twenty-nine year-old statistician
GAVRILL KUZNETZOY - a man in his late forties
VIEROCHKA KUZNEZOY - Gavrill's eighteen-year-old daughter

SETTING

A woods on a moonlit summer night.

TIME

Turn of the century Russia.

(IVAN and GAVRILL slowly walk on, chatting. IVAN carries a leather bag full of books.)

IVAN. My friend, you needn't walk any further…

(IVAN puts down his bag.)

GAVRILL. I can walk on a bit more.

IVAN. It's late, Gavrill, and I know this is about the time you like to go to bed.

GAVRILL. I know, but I feel so bad saying goodbye. It's been such a good month working with you.

IVAN. It's been just as pleasant a time for me. I'll never forget your hospitality and that of your wonderful daughter. I regret I couldn't find her to say goodbye.

GAVRILL. Who knows where she is? She goes out and comes home at will now. Who knows the mind of an eighteen year old?

IVAN. You should be proud to have a bright self-sufficient daughter.

GAVRILL. I should…

IVAN. Please, tell her I spoke of her fondly and say goodbye for me.

GAVRILL. I will do so.

IVAN. Thank you.

GAVRILL. She's a worry to me, Ivan. Vierochka has such outlandish ideas about life. But I dismiss them as the pangs of youth.

IVAN. Oh?

GAVRILL. Yes. She says people here are boring.

IVAN. Boring?

GAVRILL. Yes and that they will live and die in this little backwater town without knowing how wide this world is. Provincial she calls us.

IVAN. I'm sure she'll settle down and marry and will give you a slew of grandchildren.

GAVRILL. I hope so.

IVAN. She will…She's a wonderful girl.

GAVRILL. Thank you, but I'm holding you up with leg irons of my chatter.

IVAN. Not at all, Gavrill. No.

GAVRILL. Well…I say to you, Ivan Ogniov, anytime you need to be in this area again, you're welcome in my home.

IVAN. Thank you, Gavrill.

GAVRILL. Oh, I know it's not probable that you'll be back in these parts, but, well…you know you'd be welcome.

IVAN. I will always remember you as a man of good will. The statistics that you've helped me gather – God only knows – I would never have collected all this railroad data alone – not this quickly anyway.

GAVRILL. My pleasure. In any case send me your address in Saint Petersburg. Who knows if the raft of fate will ever carry me there.

IVAN. I will do that, friend, as soon as I arrive.

GAVRILL. Thank you, Ivan, and God bless you…

(The two men embrace. Then **GAVRILL** *slowly exits, turning to wave one final time before going off. A beat.* **IVAN** *picks up his satchel of books and is about to continue on his way when he hears a sound.)*

VIEROCHKA. *(off)* Psst….Psst…

IVAN. Who's there? I say, who's there?

*(***VIEROCHKA***, a pretty girl, enters.)*

VIEROCHKA. It's me, Ivan…

IVAN. Vierochka, what…what on earth are you doing out on this lonely road at night?

VIEROCHKA. The moon's out full…The woods aren't so dark.

IVAN. That's true…Actually, I'm glad you're here.

VIEROCHKA. You are, Ivan? You really are?

IVAN. Why wouldn't I be?

VIEROCHKA. I see…

IVAN. I looked all over for you to give you a hug and say goodbye. I even searched the carriage house and the barn.

VIEROCHKA. I'd hoped you would.

IVAN. You did?

VIEROCHKA. Yes, I did.

IVAN. Well, I wanted to thank you for all those delectable meals you cooked. You're an artist with herbs and spices. And I will miss your pastries…

VIEROCHKA. I…I enjoyed making dinners for you. I would watch you eat…watch your reaction when you tasted something new I made. You looked so amazed that food could taste so good.

IVAN. I was amazed. My talent at preparing food is putting cheese between bread slices. But…well…all good times go so fast. Bad times last forever…So…well…I suppose I'll say goodbye to you here…

VIEROCHKA. It's early…Much too early…to go back to town…to a rented room.

IVAN. I do need to settle accounts with the landlord. Then I have to pack my trunk…you know…I have to be up early tomorrow to catch the train…But, as I said, I'm glad I ran into you, Vierochka. And once again, thank you for your hospitality.

VIEROCHKA. Saint Petersburg…

IVAN. Yes, Saint Petersburg…

VIEROCHKA. Think of that…A genius at statistics and a man of the world…Going to Saint Petersburg…Isn't that a wonder.

IVAN. Saint Petersburg isn't the whole world, Vierochka.

VIEROCHKA. Compared to here, it is…Why, Saint Petersburg is called the Venice of the North. I looked it up.

IVAN. But I won't be sailing the canals all day. I'll be working.

VIEROCHKA. More statistical work for the government.

IVAN. I'll be there a while and after Saint Petersburg...who knows where...So...then...

VIEROCHKA. So...

IVAN. So I say farewell to you, Vierochka.

(*He gives a friendly hug.*)

VIEROCHKA. Why did you never call me Vera?

(**IVAN** *breaks the hug.*)

IVAN. Why didn't I...

VIEROCHKA. Yes. My father calls me Vera. But you never picked up the name.

IVAN. Vera...

VIEROCHKA. Yes...I love hearing you say it. Say it again...

IVAN. Vera...All right...Vera, I will remember you always...

VIEROCHKA. No. Stay...You call me Vera for the first time and just like that you're ready to walk away?

IVAN. It's getting late now and...

VIEROCHKA. Sit...

IVAN. Sit?...

VIEROCHKA. Sit in the moonlight and look at the face in the moon. It's smiling down on us, Ivan.

(*They sit.*)

VIEROCHKA. Moonlight...Yes, moonlight is a special light, Ivan Ogniov. It's the illumination of the heavens on us mortals.

IVAN. Oh?

VIEROCHKA. Yes, and some say you can see more of mankind in this light than in the sunlight at its noonday peak...

IVAN. Is that so?

VIEROCHKA. Yes.

IVAN. That's a poet's way of looking at this light. And a poet's way is always better than the scientific explanation that this light is just the sunlight reflecting from the moon.

VIEROCHKA. But this is a night for poetry, Ivan.

IVAN. Is that why you're out here tonight to absorb the poetry of the moon?

VIEROCHKA. Summer nights such as this are to be savored, I think.

IVAN. Oh?

VIEROCHKA. Yes, then in Winter when the drafts cut right through window glass to chill you, you can recall a night like this and take solace that Summer will come again...Besides...

IVAN. Besides what?

VIEROCHKA. Ivan, don't you think that this...this moment is romantic?...Ivan?

IVAN. Romantic...

VIEROCHKA. Sitting in the lap of a summer night, a man and a woman talking...talking intimately...

IVAN. Intimately...Are we talking...

VIEROCHKA. Yes. Sometimes I think a man and a woman talking like this intently and honestly is one of the most intimate things two people can do.

IVAN. Well, I...I...I always try to talk honestly with everyone I talk to and I...

VIEROCHKA. But you and Father talked about statistics and what conclusions can be drawn from such mathematics...It's not like this. You never sat and talked with Father about moonlight.

IVAN. No. You're right, Vera. If I were sitting here with your father...well...first we wouldn't be sitting so close and, yes, we would probably not speak of the beauty of moonlight.

VIEROCHKA. Father wouldn't even notice the moon.

IVAN. Well, I know what you're getting at, Vera, I do. And you're right...One hundred percent correct...Yes... Sitting here in this...this atmosphere...Well...I'm thinking...

VIEROCHKA. Thinking what? Tell me...Tell me...Tell me, Ivan.

IVAN. I'm just thinking...I'm 29 years of age and I've never had a romance. Not a single one. What I know of romance is only what I hear others speak of...sometimes in a coach on a train...I might, Vera, be...well...sort of unusual...

VIEROCHKA. I can't understand why you never had a romance.

IVAN. No?

VIEROCHKA. No. A young man with a good career...My God, a job that allows him to travel all over. Why would such a man never have had a romance?

IVAN. I don't know why. But I think...I think a thing like romance happens when it happens. There's no way to predict the probability of romance. And one cannot will romance to happen. No.

(*Pause.* **VIEROCHKA** *rises.*)

Vera? Vera, have I said something wrong? You've gotten so...so quiet.

VIEROCHKA. I suppose...

IVAN. (*rising*) Maybe...Maybe you're tired and should be getting back home.

(*He picks up his satchel of books.*)

VIEROCHKA. No.

IVAN. No? Your father might be worried.

VIEROCHKA. He knows I can take care of myself.

IVAN. I'm looking at you and I'm thinking.

VIEROCHKA. Again? Again you're thinking?

IVAN. Yes.

VIEROCHKA. You are? You really are this time. Tell me what you're thinking this time.

IVAN. I'm thinking...I'm imagining rather...I'm imagining you in ten years.

VIEROCHKA. Oh? And what do you see, Ivan Ogniov?

IVAN. I imagine us meeting and, yes, you are the proud mother of four beautiful children. One in a coach, three walking beside you.

VIEROCHKA. Go on.

IVAN. Well…And I see myself…

VIEROCHKA. Yes, where?

IVAN. I see myself as a well-known statistician. Yes. And we meet.

VIEROCHKA. We meet ten years from now?

IVAN. Yes, and we talk and, you know, we won't even recall this date or this day that we parted company under the reflected sunlight from the moon that lets us see each other, as you say, so clearly now. Yes, in ten years you will change. I will change. Time polishes us like pebbles tossing in the sea. We'll never again be as we are tonight…Vera?

VIEROCHKA. That's it?

IVAN. That's what I imagined…what?

VIEROCHKA. That's what you imagine as our future? We will change? Pebbles? I'll be packing around four bawling children and you'll be a renowned data collector? You imagine nothing else?

IVAN. Vera, what's the matter? Don't you feel well?…

VIEROCHKA. This is horrible…This is just one horrible night.

IVAN. Horrible?

VIEROCHKA. Yes. High on the ladder horrible, Ivan Ogniov. That's how horrible.

IVAN. This is such a turn of mood in you, Vera.

VIEROCHKA. I came out here tonight to catch you alone.

IVAN. To catch me…

VIEROCHKA. So I could speak to you.

IVAN. And we have been speaking. So what's turned you angry?

VIEROCHKA. You have made this awkward. This is not how I thought tonight would turn out.

IVAN. Vera, what are you talking about?

VIEROCHKA. What've I been…Have you been under the same moon tonight as I am?

IVAN. Vera?

VIEROCHKA. Have you been listening?

IVAN. I'm listening…

VIEROCHKA. It's just that this is so wrong to hold inside. It pains me to hold it inside…

IVAN. Say what you will, Vera. Whatever it is, I'll give you my best advice.

VIEROCHKA. Ivan Ogniov…I love you…

(VIEROCHKA *begins to cry.* IVAN *drops his bag and books spill out.*)

VIEROCHKA. I had to tell you. It…It had to be said…The night demanded it, Ivan…Ivan?

IVAN. I don't know what to say. I'm sorry. I just don't know what to say…I'm just…I'm just…

VIEROCHKA. I feel better that I've spoken my heart.

IVAN. I'm…I'm…I'm happy…happy that you're feeling better…That you said…That you said…what…what you needed to say…That you said…well, you know what you said…

VIEROCHKA. Yes, I do. I said it and now the burden is on you, Ivan Ogniov.

IVAN. The burden is on me?

VIEROCHKA. Of course…

IVAN. What does that mean? What burden is on me?

VIEROCHKA. When a woman tells a man she loves him, she gives him her heart and in that moonlit moment the world is forever changed…

IVAN. Vierochka…

VIEROCHKA. Vera…

IVAN. Listen to me…Women to me have always been…have always been something that cannot be measured or, for that matter, fathomed…That's why at this time, I don't know what to say to this…this whiplash declaration…a somewhat serious declaration…

VIEROCHKA. Yes, it is.

IVAN. You have taken me by surprise, Vierochka.

VIEROCHKA. Vera…All these weeks you've been coming to my home and eating my suppers and drinking Father's wine and telling of your travels, well…at first I admired your intelligence. I looked forward to your company from the time I got up in the morning…God, tonight, when I heard it would be your last night, while you and Father packed up your record books, I went to the foyer and I…I touched your jacket…I rubbed the sleeve across my lips, Ivan, to feel it close to me. I knew then that I could never love anyone else.

IVAN. Vierochka…

VIEROCHKA. Vera…

IVAN. My jacket?…You…you…

VIEROCHKA. Yes…Yes…

IVAN. To your lips…

VIEROCHKA. I imagined it was you, Ivan…Love is tantalizing, Ivan.

IVAN. I understand…

VIEROCHKA. However, I said it and I repeat: now the burden is on you.

IVAN. What is this burden you speak of?

VIEROCHKA. Well, you must respond to a heart given to you. It is a woman's greatest gift to a man. My heart is yours.

IVAN. This is so unexpected. And in the morning, I leave for Saint Petersburg. So what kind of response could I have? Vierochka?

VIEROCHKA. Ivan, take me with you.

IVAN. Take you?…

VIEROCHKA. You would make me the happiest woman in all of Russia.

IVAN. How could you…

VIEROCHKA. Wherever you go – to Siberia even – I'd follow. I'll be a good wife to you, Ivan. I promise. A good helpmate. A ready lover and a lifelong friend…

IVAN. Lifelong?…

VIEROCHKA. Yes…

IVAN. What about your father? He's a widower.

VIEROCHKA. He'll be happy if I'm to be married. I know he will…Later, he can even come to live with us.

IVAN. So you're saying…

VIEROCHKA. Yes, I am. You understand me perfectly. Oh, Ivan, I'm tired of this rustic nightmare of small town life. I know it will be hard for us the first few months or so, but I don't care. I think suffering and struggle shapes people into strong human beings.

IVAN. You do…

VIEROCHKA. I do…

> (**VIEROCHKA** *crosses upstage and pulls out two suit-cases.*)

Look, I have my things packed and ready.

> (*Pause.* **IVAN** *stares.*)

Ivan?

IVAN. Vierochka…

VIEROCHKA. Vera.

IVAN. I am flattered…Truly, I am…Truly…And I feel…I feel…

VIEROCHKA. Go on, Ivan. Tell me how you feel…

IVAN. I think I deserve no such feelings from one so dear as you…

VIEROCHKA. A woman stands before you with her suitcases packed and her heart in your hands and you…you…

IVAN. Vierochka Kuznetzoy, there must be mutual feelings in an equation such as you propose.

VIEROCHKA. This is not an equation, Ivan. You're standing under our moon of romance and saying…saying…

IVAN. I'm saying I admire you and I think you are beautiful, but that I…

VIEROCHKA. You admire my father, too. I heard you tell him that at supper tonight and in that exact tone of voice. I give you my heart and you give me mere admiration. That doesn't even come close.

IVAN. Doesn't come close to what?

VIEROCHKA. To a feeling! To a passion! To love, Ivan! I thought you cared for me, but were too much of a mathematician to figure out how to add moonlight and fireflies and a girl who gave over her heart and I thought you'd come up with the right answer. So I did the calculation for you.

IVAN. Vierochka, I'm sorry. I'm sort of unraveled right now.

VIEROCHKA. Unraveled?

IVAN. Yes. A man…A man cannot force himself into romance.

VIEROCHKA. Force himself?

IVAN. I mean to say…I don't know what I mean…

VIEROCHKA. Who asked you to force yourself?

IVAN. I said, I don't know what I'm saying…

VIEROCHKA. No. You do know what you're saying. Yes. One does not force love. Just as one does not force springtime or butterflies to fly or the moon to glow or…

*(****VIEROCHKA*** *begins to cry. Then she picks up her suitcases and runs off, leaving* **IVAN** *alone in the moonlight.)*

IVAN. *(calling)* Vierochka! Vierochka!

(pause)

The girl has confused me…I was in such a pleasant mood…She…Vierochka…and this…this moonlight… God, I feel bad…

(As he repacks his data books, the light slowly fade.)

She's upset it all…She's made it a night of…of…downright discomfort…She's put a burden on me all right. Yes, she has…Now instead of packing my trunk tonight in joy…I will pack my things in…in misery…pure misery…Vierochka…

CHEKHOV. Will the torture of love and youth ever stop? I think not. And poor Ivan Ogniov...Well, he finally had a first romance, even if it turned out to be Vierochka's...From the romance of a summer's night, let's go on to *The Actress*. Oh, what a reputation stage actresses have...

THE ACTRESS

CHARACTERS

PASHA SAVICH - an actress in her forties
MICHEL KALPOKOV - a man about pasha's age
MRS. KALPOKOV - Michel's wife, a woman in her mid-thirties

SETTING

Pasha Savich's apartment.

TIME

Turn of the century Russia.

*(**MICHEL KALPOKOV** lies on a sofa. **PASHA SAVICH** massages his shoulders.)*

MICHEL. Ah…Ah…Yes…That feels so, so good, Pasha… You have just the right touch for me…

PASHA. It feels good to make you feel good, my dear Michel…

*(**MICHEL** offers **PASHA** a cigarette. She takes it. He puts a cigarette in his mouth, and as he lights the match there is an insistent knock on the door. **MICHEL** blows out the match and rises.)*

MICHEL. Who in the hell is that at this hour?

PASHA. I can't imagine.

(The knock is heard again, louder this time.)

MICHEL. You'd better answer it, Pasha. I'll hide in the bedroom.

*(**MICHEL** grabs his shirt and jacket and exits. A third time the knock comes, almost desperate now. **PASHA** rushes to the door and opens it.)*

PASHA. Yes?

*(A woman, **MRS. KALPOKOV**, pushes past her and looks around. **PASHA** follows her)*

PASHA. Excuse me, Madame, you have no right to just…

MRS. KALPOKOV. Yes, I do. I need to speak with you.

PASHA. Why with me?

MRS. KALPOKOV. You are Pasha Savich…

PASHA. Yes, I am…

MRS. KALPOKOV. Then it's you I need to see.

PASHA. But I don't know you. I don't recognize you.

MRS. KALPOKOV. You wouldn't.

PASHA. So then why are you…

MRS. KALPOKOV. I have seen you on the stage.

PASHA. Oh, well, thank you. But I'm kind of busy right now. Perhaps another time if you care to talk about the theater, we could go to the tearoom and we could…

MRS. KALPOKOV. The theater is a vile place.

PASHA. Oh? Then why do you go?

MRS. KALPOKOV. My husband drags me along when he goes.

PASHA. I don't understand.

MRS. KALPOKOV. Is my husband here?

PASHA. Your husband?

MRS. KALPOKOV. Oh, don't start with your surprise act. I've seen that already on stage. That fake surprise. Well, there's no spotlight on you now, Pasha Savich. This is real.

PASHA. Who are you?

MRS. KALPOKOV. I am Mrs. Kalpokov. Again I ask, is my husband, Michel here?

PASHA. You are…

MRS. KALPOKOV. That is right. Michel Kalpokov is my husband. Where is he?

PASHA. I'm not…I'm not sure I know your husband.

MRS. KALPOKOV. You must have nerves of steel to stand there and tell me you don't know Michel.

PASHA. I don't think you have the right person, Mrs. Kalpokov.

MRS. KALPOKOV. I don't believe you are acting now. No. Now you are just out and out lying.

PASHA. Now you see here…

MRS. KALPOKOV. A liar! I'm not reluctant to say it to your face.

PASHA. What gives you the right…

MRS. KALPOKOV. I've seen you together!

PASHA. You've seen…You've seen…

MRS. KALPOKOV. Yes, I have.

PASHA. Oh…

MRS. KALPOKOV. Now stop the lying and the acting, as if there were any difference between the two. Where is he?

PASHA. Mrs. Kalpokov, as you can see, I am here alone.

MRS. KALPOKOV. In that case I will deal with you.

PASHA. About what?

MRS. KALPOKOV. Michel's been skimming money from his company…

PASHA. Your husband's stealing?

MRS. KALPOKOV. Yes.

PASHA. What has that to do with me?

MRS. KALPOKOV. If the police are called in and he's reported, they will jail Michel.

PASHA. Jail…

MRS. KALPOKOV. Oh, yes. He never did anything like this before. No. But because of the likes of you…

PASHA. The likes of me?

MRS. KALPOKOV. Don't deny it…

PASHA. Deny what? I'm sorry for your troubles, Mrs. Kalpokov, but I know nothing about this.

MRS. KALPOKOV. Not directly perhaps, no. But the likes of you, a loose…a loose woman, such as you are, caused my Michel to fall from a virtuous life.

PASHA. I should throw you out of here. Barging in and throwing sharp insults like knives. And for what reason?

MRS. KALPOKOV. Do you believe that souls burn in hell? Do you?

PASHA. I don't know if they do or if…

MRS. KALPOKOV. Oh, they do. God guarantees it, Pasha Savich. And God and I will see you down there for every night I've lain awake drenched in tears…

(MRS. KALPOKOV *cries.*)

PASHA. Mrs. Kalpokov…Please…Here…Take a handkerchief…Honestly, I don't know anything about anyone stealing money…You must believe that at least…

MRS. KALPOKOV. You think a proud man like Michel would reveal his degradation to you? Never. I know he sees you. He fell for you the first time he saw you on the stage. How he applauded you. God! So wide and hard his hands went, he almost struck my face. The second play you were in his eyes got as big as walnuts. When he's engrossed in a woman he plays with his lip, twists it. I sat next to him. I saw him twisting his lip every time you made an entrance. You up there with exaggerated make up, low cut dress. The false glitter of prop jewelry…You…You never changed a diaper or nursed one of Michel's sick children…You…You just want to parade in a stage light for men to gawk at and to yearn for…that…that phony stage fantasy…that is your existence…

PASHA. Listen, Mrs. Kalpokov, all women suffer. Oh, yes, we all do. Last month an army officer that I…well…entertained beat me for no reason. A captain in the Tsar's army beat me…

MRS. KALPOKOV. It's not the same…It's not the same as what I'm suffering now. It's just not…

PASHA. Please stop crying. I…I do have many guests… visitors…I don't have an apple tree and three boys to climb it. Yes, I regret it, but that's not the turn my life took. And when the stage lights go dark, loneliness lights up inside me…So…So, yes…I fill my life up with acquaintances…Michel…Your husband is not my prisoner…He's free to come and go…

MRS. KALPOKOV. But it was for you that he did what he did. Stealing the money.

PASHA. For me?

MRS. KALPOKOV. Yes. He had to have the means to act like a man about town, a *bon vivant.*

PASHA. Mrs. Kalpokov, I didn't know anything about this stolen money. I'm hearing it from you for the first time.

MRS. KALPOKOV. You are still Michel's near occasion of sin.

PASHA. I…

MRS. KALPOKOV. Don't you see? Do you care? Does your kind care? Does your kind ever consider that such guests as you call them have wives and children and responsibilities? If Michel's turned in, they'll send him to prison. The children and I will tumble into a pit of poverty.

PASHA. Oh, my, no. Don't say that. God forbid.

MRS. KALPOKOV. Then help me. I made an arrangement with Michel's supervisor.

PASHA. An arrangement?

MRS. KALPOKOV. Yes. If I return the 1500 rubles that Michel skimmed, Michel will just be discharged and he'll be free to find another position. If the 1500 is not returned, the constabulary will be brought in.

PASHA. I see…

MRS. KALPOKOV. I need the 1500 rubles today…

PASHA. Today…

MRS. KALPOKOV. Well?

PASHA. Are you…Are you asking me for…for…

MRS. KALPOKOV. Yes. Fifteen hundred rubles…

PASHA. But I received none of that money you speak of. None.

MRS. KALPOKOV. I don't believe he handed you cash. No. So I'm asking…asking…

PASHA. For what?

MRS. KALPOKOV. I know about women who have – shall we say – your life style. They…They require gifts… Expensive gifts…From your gentleman friends…All I'm asking is that in this time of crisis – family crisis – that you return to me only those gifts that my husband gave you…I know a merchant who buys such items. In this way I can repay the 1500 rubles to Michel's employer.

PASHA. The only problem with your plan, Mrs. Kalpokov, is that Michel hasn't given me any gifts that valuable.

MRS. KALPOKOV. What is this?

PASHA. What is what? Your husband has never given me anything of great value…No, I'm sorry.

MRS. KALPOKOV. Then where in God's name is the money?

PASHA. I don't know.

MRS. KALPOKOV. If you're holding back because I said some rude things to you, you have to overlook them. Pasha Savich, I'm at my wit's end. You see before you a woman, a wife, in pain. But I need to sell those items he gave you to save my family. Please…I beg you… If you have any decency left, please, give me what he brought to endear himself to you…I'm begging you now…

(**PASHA** *crosses to a small table, opens a drawer and removes a jewelry box. She takes a thin bracelet and a plain ring. She crosses back to* **MRS. KALPOKOV.**)

PASHA. These are the two items that Michel gave me. If you like, they're yours.

(**MRS. KALPOKOV** *takes the jewelry.*)

MRS. KALPOKOV. These?

PASHA. Those are what your husband gave me.

MRS. KALPOKOV. Why these wouldn't bring anywhere near the amount I need. These are…are trinkets…

PASHA. I'm sorry…I can see you're in a quandary. I know when a woman is in an impossible situation…Trust me, I do…Why do you look at me like that?…I swear to heaven these are his gifts to me…

MRS. KALPOKOV. But…I…I've seen you out with Michel…

PASHA. So you said.

MRS. KALPOKOV. I peered into the restaurant where he likes to take you…

PASHA. You have?

MRS. KALPOKOV. I have. My stomach burned to see you together…I'm a ruin of a woman over this…

PASHA. I'm so sorry…I didn't mean for anyone to be hurt…

MRS. KALPOKOV. You were well dressed and you wore a beautiful broach on your left shoulder and an exquisite diamond bracelet. That's the jewelry I thought Michel gave you.

PASHA. The broach was from the director of my last play and the bracelet was from the army captain…No… Michel gave me only these pieces you hold in your hand. On other occasions he merely brought me wine or chocolates. That's all.

MRS. KALPOKOV. Dining at expensive restaurants. Wine. Chocolates. And at home the children eat bread and butter. Oh, God, tell me what to do. What? If I don't raise the 1500 rubles, we're ruined.

(**MRS. KALPOKOV** *cries again.*)

PASHA. Maybe…Maybe you'd like a cup of tea or a…

MRS. KALPOKOV. No…Nothing…Listen to me. I'm begging – I've never begged in my life – now listen to me begging – you have corrupted my husband and now you must give him a chance to be reclaimed by virtue and the grace of the Almighty. Only you can save my Michel…

PASHA. Despite what you think of me, I don't want to see anyone's family destroyed…But what do you want of me?

MRS. KALPOKOV. I will get down on my knees…

(*She kneels.*)

PASHA. Please, don't…please get up…Mrs. Kalpokov…

MRS. KALPOKOV. I beg you to help me help him…and his children… (*She cries again.*) Please…Oh, God…

PASHA. I can take no more of this! No more!

(PASHA crosses back to the table and picks up her jewelry box. She crosses back to MRS. KALPOKOV, who is still crying.)

PASHA. Here…This is all the jewelry I have. None of it is from your husband, but everything is yours, even the broach and the bracelet you found so exquisite.

MRS. KALPOKOV. *(rising)* You're giving me…

PASHA. Everything…The whole jewelry box. Go look in the drawer yourself. It's everything. As long as you realize that none of this comes from stolen money or any other money belonging to Michel Kalpokov. So, go… They're worth much more than 1500 rubles…

MRS. KALPOKOV. Yes…Yes…They are…

PASHA. Also know before you go off to sell my jewelry that I did not entice Michel to come here. No. He came here to see me because he wanted to…Go now…Go save your family…

(MRS. KALPOKOV wraps the jewelry in her scarf and hands the box back to PASHA.)

MRS. KALPOKOV. I don't understand how you can live like this. I never will. I think you will come to a bad end… Goodbye…

(MRS. KALPOKOV runs off. After a beat, MICHEL enters. He is dressed now.)

PASHA. Michel, I'm sorry you heard all that.

MICHEL. She begged…She begged…

PASHA. She was upset…

MICHEL. She begged. She cried. She debased herself here in…in an actress's apartment…In an actress's apartment…

PASHA. What?

MICHEL. You heard me. The mother of my children on her knees before…before you, Pasha Savich…

PASHA. But I never asked her to…

MICHEL. On her knees before a stage actress…My wife… She's my wife, Pasha. Do you understand?

PASHA. Michel?

MICHEL. I am so damned ashamed. So…So…ashamed… And so should you be…You hear me…Do you?

*(**MICHEL** runs out the front door. After a beat, **PASHA** puts the empty jewelry box away, as the lights fade.)*

PASHA. He was a captain in our own Russian army. He loved the play. He had such a wonderful time up here. And for no reason…he beat me…

CHEKHOV. In some stories as in life, it's not so easy to pick the victim or the villain. All experience is just a perspective, and sometimes truth becomes lost in the tangle of perspectives. For an even more tangled situation, I'd like you to meet a woman named Olga Ivanovna…

OLGA'S DOCTOR

43

CHARACTERS

OLGA IVANOVA - a woman in her thirties
DR. NIKOLAI TSWYTKOV - a medical doctor in his forties

SETTING

A modestly appointed living room.

TIME

Turn of the century Russia.

(**OLGA IVANOVNA** *looks out at the audience. She wipes tears away. After a beat,* **DOCTOR NIKOLAI TSWYTKOV** *enters from the bedroom. He carries a small doctor's case. He stops.* **OLGA** *turns and looks at him.*)

OLGA. How did you find him tonight?…Nikolai?

NIKOLAI. He's resting…

OLGA. What my son's going through can't be called rest. I think…I think he just shuts his eyes to the terror…

NIKOLAI. But at the moment he rests…

OLGA. Life is meaningless without that boy, Nikolai. He's the only truth in my life. And I am helpless to do anything.

NIKOLAI. Olga, may I get you something?

OLGA. No, thank you. Nothing would help. If I…If I lose him, my Misa…If I…If I cease to be a mother, I will become the last curl of smoke from a spent candle. Misa's doom would be mine…

NIKOLAI. Olga, sit…

OLGA. I don't want to sit. My body's kicking at its own walls. I can't sit. (*pause*) When Misa was born…

NIKOLAI. Don't grind those memories into yourself…

OLGA. How can I not recall? You're a doctor, Nikolai. You know the brain is a vault of memories. And I'm locked inside with all of them. Now the memories grow bigger like storm waves at sea. I sent my son away to be adopted. How could I have done such harshness to Misa? Who was that woman, Nikolai, nine years ago, who sent her baby away? Oh, yes, I took him back in time. But I don't know that wretched Olga who…what a selfish woman she was…Some force of nature turned me into a mother. You understand, Nikolai. How can people tolerate their pasts? Tell me…

NIKOLAI. Let it be. Let the past be. Now…Yes, you are a good mother.

OLGA. I'm scared, Nikolai…

NIKOLAI. Yes…

OLGA. Of you. I'm frightened by you.

NIKOLAI. I scare you?

OLGA. You do. You just came from his room, just as you have been every night for weeks and you have not given me one hopeful word.

NIKOLAI. Olga, I…

OLGA. I can sense it. You've given up hope. But I will not give up hope. I won't…You look at me as if you want me to. Do you?

NIKOLAI. I'd love more than anything to be able to give you hope. But dear Olga, I'm not a priest, I'm a doctor.

OLGA. It's that bad? When people speak of priests it's close to the end. I can see in your eyes, you think that.

NIKOLAI. There is a terror being in medicine. The terror is that we are helpless in moments such as these. Misa's tumor has not diminished. It seems to be larger and pressuring the boy's brain further. I've used every procedure known to science to reverse this growth. I've consulted with the best doctors, my colleagues at the university. Now…at this stage…only sedatives give the boy some relief. That's why he's resting now.

OLGA. And you're absolutely certain. That's what scares me. God…

NIKOLAI. Anything hopeful I would say would be a falsehood.

OLGA. Nikolai…

NIKOLAI. I'm only being blunt because…Well…Olga, listen to me. We must prepare ourselves for what's to be. I'm so, so sorry to say that…

OLGA. Did he say he felt worse? Nikolai? What did Misa say to you tonight?

NIKOLAI. I asked if he was feeling any better and he…he said, no. He said he just keeps dreaming…

OLGA. That's what he tells me…Dreaming…Dreaming of nursery rhymes coming to life. The nursery rhymes I used to read to him…He…He remembers…

NIKOLAI. He said his head ached. I said, well, young man, we all become sick now and then. That's the human lot. Then…Then I gave him his sedative and he shut his eyes.

OLGA. Oh, my Misa…

NIKOLAI. All I can do now is try to…try to prepare you for…

OLGA. Don't say it…Just don't…Please…

NIKOLAI. Olga…

OLGA. What about some of those university doctors you consulted? Suppose one of them came here to examine Misa?

NIKOLAI. I asked you weeks ago if you wanted to consult another doctor.

OLGA. That was then. This is now.

NIKOLAI. I'll arrange it. I'll bring the head of the medical school. I'll call on him tonight and tomorrow I'll have him look at Misa…

OLGA. If Misa's in pain, why…why doesn't he cry out? Why, Nikolai?

NIKOLAI. I sense he doesn't want to upset you anymore than you are…

(**OLGA** *wipes away tears.*)

OLGA. God…God is punishing me, because when Misa was born I did not appreciate the miracle that God wrought in my womb.

NIKOLAI. God has the puppet strings of all humanity to pull, but I like to think that God is not so cruel as to take children to punish adults.

OLGA. Then what is responsible? What good is all your medicine if it can't cure these ills? Where do we turn? What do we do? How can I go on if…if…I say "if" as if there really were an "if"…

NIKOLAI. I'll return in the morning and I'll bring with
    me...

OLGA. No one...

NIKOLAI. But you said...

OLGA. It's not necessary...I believe what you said. You are
    the best physician in the city. They all say so...I believe
    you, but I don't want to...

NIKOLAI. Then I'll be back in the morning myself. *(pause)*
    Olga, in...in this time of sorrow, which I truly share
    with you, I...I...

OLGA. What is it, Nikolai?

NIKOLAI. You told me once that Misa is my...my son. And
    now I want to know...is it true?

OLGA. What I told you...What I told you years ago...years
    ago...

NIKOLAI. Yes...I know what you told me. Olga, you're the
    only one I've ever known...The only one I've had such
    feelings for...I'm asking...What I'm asking is to tell
    me if you just said such a thing with certainty or...or...
    Look, this is a time...such a time...of sadness when
    certain truths come out between two people...Do I...
    Do I love a boy?...a good boy?...a gentle soul? Or do
    I love my own flesh and blood? Olga? Did you invent
    such a story or...or is...a father has rights Olga...

OLGA. Stop it...Misa is...is...

NIKOLAI. Is what?

OLGA. Is yours...

NIKOLAI. Lies wound people. I can see...your tears mag-
    nify your eyes, Olga...I see someone lying even now.
    You who have been the one love of my life that I cher-
    ished...Oh, yes, you were carefree then and ran from
    party to party like a girl on fire with life...But I saw
    through that wild streak of youth to the intelligent
    person underneath...Olga, hear me...I am getting
    older now and I often dwell on our time together as
    a happy moment...I thought I was special to you...I
    thought...

OLGA. Nikolai…

NIKOLAI. Then in the jungle of youth…I lost you…I don't know what happened…Tell me…Tell me why this stubborn will to hold fast to this lie? Olga, it plagues my peace of mind…

OLGA. Nikolai, you asked me and I answered you. Then you accuse me of…

NIKOLAI. Petros, the furrier!…

OLGA. Petros…

NIKOLAI. And Kurovsky, the playboy!…Both of them send you money for Misa, the same as I do…

OLGA. You…You spoke with…

NIKOLAI. Yes. It's a small city, Olga. People talk and talk pours its way like lava through the streets. So, yes, we got together…Petros and Kurovsky and I…

OLGA. I see…

NIKOLAI. You do? All these years you collected money from three different men you claimed as fathers to that boy in there…Now with the boy nearing the end…

OLGA. Nikolai…

NIKOLAI. Nearing the end…now even now you try to keep juggling the balls, Olga.

OLGA. Nikolai, don't think ill of me. Not you. Not now.

NIKOLAI. What can anyone think? Petros even kept the letter you sent him telling him Misa was his.

OLGA. No…

NIKOLAI. He showed me the letter, Olga…It was in your hand…Nine years ago when a poor but pretty woman who thought the world to be one long endless party became pregnant. You started this. It seems…It was all about the money, wasn't it? Stop staring at me and tell me. Please, tell me. Is the boy mine?

(**OLGA** *sits and stares.* **NIKOLAI** *crosses to sit beside her.*)

Oh, God, forgive me, Olga. At a time like this…All the loathsome words I said…I apologize, Olga…I regret my tone of voice…I should've kept my head…I'm sorry…

OLGA. I'm sorry, too, Nikolai…

NIKOLAI. I just…I just wanted to know if my son is dying…
That's all…My feelings are raw also.

OLGA. Don't ask me anything more…I'm just surviving…
living the only way I know how, Nikolai…A young girl
pregnant in a small city like this…Who could a girl
turn to?

NIKOLAI. You dropped out of sight…No one could find
you…

OLGA. My mother in shame kept me at home…until…

NIKOLAI. But you knew I cared for you and that I would…

OLGA. You would do what? You were in medical school…
And what if you weren't? Your family would've shunned
me. Your sisters both hated me…

NIKOLAI. Jealous of your beauty…I remember…

OLGA. Then with my mother passing away. God, I had no
means…None…The others – Petros and Kurovsky –
were too concerned for their families' reputations…
In a panic, at his birth I brought him to the nuns so
they could give Misa to a barren family…Then I had a
change of heart and took my Misa back…But if I were
to raise the boy myself, I'd need money, so…so…Here
I am…Olga Ivanovna…Have some pity on her…her
folly…

(**NIKOLAI** *rises and puts on his coat.*)

NIKOLAI. So you, in truth, don't know who the father is?…
Olga?…All right…So be it…I'll return in the morning
to look in on Misa…

(**NIKOLAI** *exits.* **OLGA** *rises.*)

OLGA. No, I don't know who Misa belongs to. I don't
know…But I never loved Petros the furrier or Kurovsky
the playboy…Them…Them…I never loved, Nikolai…
Never…Never…Never…

(*Lights fade on* **OLGA IVANOVNA.**)

CHEKHOV. In this modern age who could've found a way to traverse the emotional labyrinth of Olga Ivanovna's feelings? And why couldn't Dr. Nikolai Tswytkov ignore his family's displeasure and take Olga for his wife…Ah, nineteenth-century life…What will happen to the fallen Olga now? That would be yet another story…Next we shall listen in on the conversation between a governess, Julia Vasilevnova, and her well-to-do employer. Let's observe how he treats this young woman he calls a boob…

THE BOOB

CHARACTERS

THE EMPLOYER - a man in his late forties
JULIA VASILEVNOVA - a governess in her twenties

SETTING

A well-appointed sitting room.

TIME

Turn of the century Russia.

(**THE EMPLOYER**, *a well-dressed gentleman, paces the floor. After a beat,* **JULIA VASILEVNOVA** *enters timidly.*)

EMPLOYER. Finally…

JULIA. I'm sorry, Sir. Kolya needed some extra help with his long division.

EMPLOYER. Yes…Please, Julia, sit.

(**JULIA** *sits.*)

Today is payday…

JULIA. That's so, Sir…

EMPLOYER. Actually its five days late…

JULIA. Yes…Yes, it is…

EMPLOYER. When you started here, you said you required thirty rubles per month.

JULIA. Sir…

EMPLOYER. Well?

JULIA. I remember that you agreed to forty rubles per month.

EMPLOYER. Thirty. Thirty, Julia…I wrote it down somewhere…Besides I don't think a governess is worth more than thirty a month…

JULIA. It must be that I misunderstood then.

EMPLOYER. Of course you must have. Now let's see. I calculate that you've been here two months.

JULIA. Two months and five days, Sir.

EMPLOYER. Yes…You needn't have reminded me, Julia…

JULIA. I meant no disrespect, Sir. I was just saying…

EMPLOYER. Two months, which means I owe you sixty rubles.

JULIA. I suppose. Yes, Sir.

EMPLOYER. Now I need to deduct from that nine Sundays.

JULIA. Nine Sundays?

EMPLOYER. You had no duties with my Kolya or Varya on Sundays.

JULIA. No formal instruction, no...but I...

EMPLOYER. You what? What were you about to say, Julia?

JULIA. No. Nothing, Sir.

EMPLOYER. All right then. I continue calculating. In addition to Sundays when you merely kept an eye on the children, you took leave on three holidays.

JULIA. But, Sir, they were holidays.

EMPLOYER. That's what I said, isn't it?

JULIA. Yes, Sir...

EMPLOYER. There were four days when Kolya was sick with fever and you gave him no instruction on those days... You only worked with my daughter, Varya...Now also there were three days when you were ill with a cold.

JULIA. Yes, Sir. I caught it from Kolya when I read to him and I...

EMPLOYER. Be that as it may, you had no official duties, teaching duties that is, with either Kolya or Varya on those days.

JULIA. No, I did not...

EMPLOYER. So, let me see, twelve and seven is nineteen, so that's minus nineteen. That leaves you with a payday of...of just forty-one rubles.

JULIA. Forty-one...

EMPLOYER. Wait...No...There are some other deductions.

JULIA. Other deductions, Sir?

EMPLOYER. Unfortunately, yes...You'll recall on New Year's Eve, you dropped an expensive cup and saucer, but I've only deducted two rubles, because my wife's mother gave us that set and I can't stand my wife's mother.

JULIA. I see...

EMPLOYER. Then there was the other day when you fell to day dreaming, while Kolya climbed the cherry tree and tore his jacket. So minus another ten rubles to repair a leather jacket lined with wool…Also, there's the incident where you went sledding with Varya which resulted in the loss of her rabbit fur gloves…

JULIA. But Varya lost those because…

EMPLOYER. I also recall that on the tenth of this month my wife advanced you ten rubles…

JULIA. That's not accurate, Sir…

EMPLOYER. I have my notation right here.

JULIA. Your notation?

EMPLOYER. Yes…twenty-seven from forty-one equals… equals fourteen.

(**JULIA** *gasps.*)

JULIA. Your wife, Sir, only advanced me three rubles to purchase some personal items…That's all, just three rubles.

EMPLOYER. My records show an advance of ten rubles.

JULIA. No…I mean to say, Sir, perhaps there was a misunderstanding…

EMPLOYER. No. I don't think so. My wife and I are precise about our household accounts.

(**THE EMPLOYER** *counts out fourteen rubles.*)

Here you are, Julia Vasilevnova, fourteen rubles that are owed to you…

JULIA. *(rising)* Thank you…Sir…

EMPLOYER. What was that you said?

JULIA. I just said thank you, Sir…

EMPLOYER. Why?

JULIA. Sir?

EMPLOYER. Why are you thanking me? Answer…

JULIA. It is, Sir, a common courtesy to thank an employer for a salary given.

EMPLOYER. Boob!

JULIA. Sir?

EMPLOYER. You are a boob! I just stood before you and robbed you, Julia, robbed you blind for putting up with my two brats.

JULIA. Kolya and Varya?

EMPLOYER. Worst children in this neighborhood. Peerless in the world of brats. Yes, they are. And for two months and five days you have labored to teach them and guide them and tolerate their unending, unbridled tantrums. Then I short change you your meager salary and you thank me. Boob.

JULIA. I take what I'm given, Sir. That's what we do. That's how it is…

EMPLOYER. I was kidding you, Julia Vasilevnova. Jesting, to show you that you need to stand up for yourself, stand up to being bullied into submission all the time.

JULIA. So…Jesting?…

EMPLOYER. Yes… *(He takes more money out.)* Here's the rest of your eighty plus rubles that I legitimately owe you for two months and five days…

(He hands her the money.)

Take it…

(JULIA takes the money.)

I don't understand you, young woman. I've observed you since you've become governess here. Don't you ever protest anything? Yes, Sir. Yes Ma'am. Yes, Varya. Yes, Kolya. Those brats need to be yelled at and kicked in the pants.

JULIA. Sir, I can't very well behave that way and you know that. I'm not that kind of person.

EMPLOYER. I know that. It's the reason we're having this talk. Why do you want to continue to go through life like…like a boob?

JULIA. Sir…

EMPLOYER. Go on…Answer me. Why did you sit there holding back what you were obviously dying to say to me? Why?

JULIA. May I answer, Sir?

EMPLOYER. I am pleading with you to do so. Go on. Enlighten me…

JULIA. Enlighten…

EMPLOYER. Yes.

JULIA. Then I will. I am a woman, Sir. In this world that's what I am. Anything but silent suffering is deemed being uppity, not knowing one's place, if you will, Sir. You know – or should know – that a woman in my position could be dismissed from service for protesting the meanness of a man, the callousness of an employer… the jest of a supervisor. No, Sir, I am not a boob. Not at all. I am well read. I speak English and French and I can do higher mathematics. No, not a boob at all. What you don't understand – maybe what you can't understand – is that, Sir, were I a man or if I had wealth or authority, you and the world might be stunned by what I am capable of doing. I hope I have given you a satisfactory answer to your question. I hope I leave you enlightened. But now it is time to return to your Kolya and long division. Good day to you, Sir…

(*JULIA exits, as the lights fade.*)

EMPLOYER. So where has she been for two months and five days, this Julia Vasilevnova that I've met today for the first time?…Hmmm…

CHEKHOV. The poor…The poor are always weak or need to appear to be – And the rich…the rich are strong or, yes, think they are strong when the truth is they are just weaklings with wealth. Some things in life never change…Let me have you meet next Mrs. Lidocka Sarnov dressed in her pink stockings…

THE PINK STOCKINGS

CHARACTERS

LIDOCKA SARNOV - a pretty young woman
VLADIMIR SARNOV - her husband, a high school teacher

SETTING

A small study.

TIME

Turn of the century Russia.

(**LIDOCKA**, *wearing a light summer dress and pink stock-ings sits at a desk laboring over a letter she is attempting to write. After a beat, her husband,* **VLADIMIR** *enters. He looks at* **LIDOCKA**. *So engrossed is she in her writ-ing that she does not notice as he crosses behind her and looks over her shoulder at what she is writing. After read-ing some of her letter, he abruptly pulls the page from her hand.*)

LIDOCKA. Vladimir? What's the matter?

VLADIMIR. What's the matter? Look at this. Just look…

LIDOCKA. What? It's a letter I'm writing…

VLADIMIR. There are ink blots…smudges…finger prints… The lines…God…The lines…They go upward then down and then they disappear like a train that went off a cliff…

LIDOCKA. It's only a personal letter.

VLADIMIR. A letter…a letter, Lidocka?

LIDOCKA. Yes, to my sister, Anya…

VLADIMIR. Anya will have to decipher this before she can read it…And the content…

LIDOCKA. Content…

VLADIMIR. Lidocka, hen tracks have more logic to them. The ink smudges are the only interesting facets of this composition that decomposes as I go through it.

LIDOCKA. You're being much too critical of what is only…

VLADIMIR. Too critical? Too…Look, here. There's no verb in this one legible sentence…

LIDOCKA. What? Where? No verb?

VLADIMIR. *(reading)* "Vladimir his blue suit on Sunday."

LIDOCKA. Oh, my, yes, you're right there, Vladimir. I should write wore. Vladimir wore his blue suit on Sunday. Yes…I can slip in "wore." I can do that.

VLADIMIR. You don't consider this letter a waste of time?

LIDOCKA. Why is it a waste of time?

VLADIMIR. Who gives a damn about me in my blue suit on Sunday? Who?

LIDOCKA. I am just keeping Anya up to date on what we're doing.

VLADIMIR. What you're writing is of no interest to Anya or to anyone else.

LIDOCKA. I spent two hours at this desk writing, I'll have you know. Its six pages…

VLADIMIR. Six pages of blather, Lidocka. There is no evidence here of any thought whatsoever. Letter writing is – can be – an exciting art of human communication, a process that lifts us up from the common beasts of this earth. But this…

LIDOCKA. So, I'm not such a good writer.

VLADIMIR. In order to write one must have some…some meat in the narrative.

LIDOCKA. I most certainly do.

VLADIMIR. You do?

LIDOCKA. I do…

VLADIMIR. Where in this tome of vacuity? Show me… Under which smudge must I look?

LIDOCKA. Right here, on the third page, at the bottom…

VLADIMIR. *(reading)* "We're having stew today. Tuesday is always stew day." What?

LIDOCKA. You said I had no meat in my letter…

VLADIMIR. Good God, Lidocka! I'm talking about substance. Substance. I used the word meat as a metaphor for substance!

LIDOCKA. I don't know what a metaphor is. I know I should learn, so I could use metaphors in my letter to Anya…

VLADIMIR. *(reading)* "The weather has been rainy and rainy weather makes Vladimir grouchy." I am not grouchy.

LIDOCKA. Yes, you are. I can see and hear you being grouchy right now.

VLADIMIR. I was not grouchy before you showed me this…this…this travesty of penmanship and thought! Another thing: there are words spelled with letters missing…

LIDOCKA. Oh?

VLADIMIR. *(reading)* A famous pianist visited the city. Famous you spelled, F-A-M-O-S.

LIDOCKA. Oh…

VLADIMIR. Are you trying to save ink, Lidocka?

LIDOCKA. You know I'm not. I just can't spell. I guess you'll need to look at the letter and make corrections, so I can write it over.

VLADIMIR. You want me to…to spend time editing and correcting…I'd be in a wheelchair before I'd finish a job like this. It needs polish, grammar, punctuation, spelling, syntax and most of all, substance.

LIDOCKA. That poor…

VLADIMIR. I haven't eaten the stew yet and I've got indigestion. Were any of my colleagues to see such…such poverty of skill, it would, God, yes, it would embarrass me.

LIDOCKA. Vladimir…Vladimir, is that why you never take me to any of the get-togethers when they have some function at the school?

VLADIMIR. No…No…It's just that…well…my friends at the school would bore you…I go myself to those gatherings for work related reasons – that's all.

LIDOCKA. I'm sorry, Vladimir. I know I have no real education. I just wanted to write to Anya in Moscow and tell her how it is now that I'm…We're married…That's all I was trying to do…That's all…

VLADIMIR. Now I'm the one who should apologize for being so critical. It's just that with my position as a History teacher at the High School, you know what I'm saying, I just wouldn't want anyone to know how… well…how much difficulty you have writing…

LIDOCKA. But I feel ashamed. The best thing I could do is not ever write anything. In that way, I could hide... hide my...my lack of...

VLADIMIR. No. No. I don't believe that's a correct track to follow. No...Suppose – you – we have children. You should be capable of teaching them the rudiments of reading and writing before they start school.

LIDOCKA. I guess I could learn...I think I could learn...Are we going to have children, Vladimir?

VLADIMIR. I don't know. It's not the kind of thing one reads in tea leaves, Dear. If the Lord makes you fertile, you will, yes. We were speaking of you learning composition...

(**LIDOCKA** *wipes away a tear.*)

Now what? Lidocka?

LIDOCKA. Vladimir...Vladimir, do you think that...well... one of the Russian teachers at the High School would...would give me lessons?

VLADIMIR. One of the...Now how would that look for me? Right now if we happen upon one of my colleagues at the market, you act pleasant enough...Don't be too concerned, Lidocka. They don't know what you don't know. But if you were to start handing them your writings...well...

LIDOCKA. It's my mother's fault. She sent my brothers to school. But me...and Anya...she should've sent us to some sort of school instead of just teaching us to sew and cook and to...

VLADIMIR. Now, now, Lidocka...Look, the rain has stopped...

LIDOCKA. Yes, it has. I'm so happy for you, Vladimir.

VLADIMIR. You know...I think your mother was wiser than you know. You send a girl to school and make her an intellectual type and you ruin that girl, Lidocka...

LIDOCKA. You think so?

VLADIMIR. I know so. How many times at the High School have I seen it? God. The French teacher. The music teacher. The art teacher. Why, I have a friend at the school, Boris. He teaches chemistry…

LIDOCKA. Boris Kasperkov, yes, I met him at the post office.

VLADIMIR. Well his wife teaches first year music. She studied at the conservatory in Moscow.

LIDOCKA. Oh, my…

VLADIMIR. Yes – But she's constantly debating every blessed statement Boris Kasperkov makes.

LIDOCKA. She does?…

VLADIMIR. Constantly…at lunch…On the way home…In the hallways…They lack only swords and shields…

LIDOCKA. Why Vladimir would she do such a thing?

VLADIMIR. That's what I'm trying to tell you: educated women become willful and contradictory, Lidocka. They develop half-baked ideas that make no sense. They think because they attained scholarship that they've become men. For example, the women at the High School are complaining about the pay scale, because men are paid a higher wage than women…

LIDOCKA. Men should make more than women. Men are the heads of households…

VLADIMIR. If you said that at one of our lunch discussions, the women would shout you down.

LIDOCKA. I see…But, Vladimir, there's something else I don't understand…

VLADIMIR. What's that?

LIDOCKA. You go on and on about how lacking I am, but in the same conversation, you say that you don't care for these…these educated women…I'm a know-nothing, but if I did know something, I get the sense that you wouldn't like me too much…Am I right?

VLADIMIR. The rain started again…

LIDOCKA. Oh…I'm sorry, Vladimir…But did you hear what I asked?

VLADIMIR. I did…Look, Dear, you're confusing issues. I don't want to discourage you from growing your intellect, but I'm trying to explain to you that women… women are more pleasing to a man when…well… when they wear pink stockings and make a good beef stew…

LIDOCKA. They are?

VLADIMIR. Yes. Look how alluring they make your legs look…

LIDOCKA. Oh, Vladimir, you mean it?

VLADIMIR. Of course I mean it…Who asked you to buy those pink stockings?

LIDOCKA. You've got my face all red now…And I…I forget what I wanted to say…

VLADIMIR. Speak your mind, Lidocka. It sharpens one's wits to have discussions like this.

LIDOCKA. Well, I was…I was just thinking…

VLADIMIR. Yes, go on…

LIDOCKA. What if…what if you want to, say, have a conversation with an educated woman…some time? What…I mean, where would you turn? Vladimir?

VLADIMIR. Good…Good question…Simple answer…I chat with educated women every day…

LIDOCKA. You…you do?

VLADIMIR. Well, yes, I have some of the wildest conversations at lunch break…

LIDOCKA. Oh?…

VLADIMIR. Yes, with Masha and Maria and Natalie…

LIDOCKA. About what? Conversations about what?

VLADIMIR. About what…About historical movements… cultural changes…literature…School teacher kinds of conversations…

LIDOCKA. Every day…I mean, every lunch break you… you…

VLADIMIR. Almost every day. And they all marvel at the delicious spiced lunches you prepare for me…

LIDOCKA. They do? My lunches? You sit and eat my lunches and have conversations with...with...

(**LIDOCKA** *begins to cry.*)

VLADIMIR. Lidocka, what on earth are you crying about?

LIDOCKA. Vladimir...I...I...I want...

VLADIMIR. What? What do you want? Tell me. Lidocka?

LIDOCKA. I think...I think I want to start a family...

VLADIMIR. We're...we're trying...What do you think we're doing every night when we lock the dog out of our room?

LIDOCKA. I'm saying...I'm saying...I think...I think we're going to have to try harder...

VLADIMIR. All right...We'll try harder...Whatever that means...

LIDOCKA. Thank you, Vladimir...Thank you...

VLADIMIR. Not at all...

(**LIDOCKA** *crosses and picks up a book from the desk.*)

Where are you going, Lidocka?

LIDOCKA. I'm going...I'm going to read...I'm going to read and read and read, until I...until I improve my mind, Vladimir.

VLADIMIR. Lidocka, that is a history of the French Revolution...

LIDOCKA. Then that's where I'll start...with the French Revolution and then...then yes, I'll go on to every other revolution there is in the world...

(**LIDOCKA** *walks off.* **VLADIMIR** *shakes his head.* **VLADIMIR** *looks out at the audience as if looking from a window, as the lights fade.*)

VLADIMIR. The French Revolution...Lidocka...When will this damned rain stop, so I can take my dog out for a walk...When?...

CHEKHOV. How many an insecure man marries the right girl who is wrong for him? Something to dwell on. I know. Don't say it. There's a great deal of crying

women in these tales. I know. The weakness of men,
I've observed, causes most of the tears of women...
To conclude this cavalcade of nineteenth century
Russian women, I give you the events which changed
the life of one Marysyas Nemenov...And Marysyas does
not cry in her story – The Rabbit and the Snake...

THE RABBIT AND THE SNAKE

71

CHARACTERS

PETER SEMYENICH SARNOV - a young bachelor
LEON NEMENOV - a real estate broker, a couple of years older than Peter
MARYSYAS NEMENOV - the pretty wife of Leon, about Peter Semyenich's age

SETTING

Various.

TIME

Turn of the century Russia.

*(**PETER SEMYENICH** enters and addresses the audience.)*

PETER. Good evening. I am Peter Semyenich. I come before you tonight to demonstrate the art of seduction. I have no qualms about telling it, because I believe that all women, one way or another must be seduced before any man can succeed in winning their love. You see, women don't see the beauty in us men the same way we instantly see the beauty in women. So our work is slower. That's why the first point to make is that the gentleman must never, never, never rush a performance. I say performance, yes. All seduction is a *coup de theatre.* Seduction: a prologue and five acts culminating in a delectable epilogue.

Next, yes, would be to tell the analogy of the snake and the rabbit: The snake's eyes mesmerize the rabbit and hold the rabbit's life in its gaze. But, alas, how does a man mesmerize a lady? Listen to me. There are indifferent husbands all over Russia. Thus, whenever you find a desirable woman with an indifferent husband, you simply employ his apathy in your hunt. Let him do the work for you. For example, I love – I mean I have fallen from a high cliff into an ocean of love with – Marysyas Nemenov...

*(A light comes up on the beautiful **MARYSYAS** in a freeze.)*

Have you ever seen the beauty of God's world so boldly stated? I have not. I dream of this delicate rabbit with a devotion that makes the heart race and the hands tremble...

*(A light comes up on **LEON NEMENOV**, also in a freeze.)*

This, my friends, is her husband, Leon Nemenov. Oh, a fine enough man, but guilty of the mortal sin of not truly appreciating his wife's assets.

(PETER crosses to LEON.)

PETER*(cont.)*. One night at the theater during intermission, I begin my quest…

(LEON unfreezes.)

(to LEON) And how is Marysyas?

LEON. Marysyas? You know, as always…She's just the same old Marysyas…

PETER. Surely, you're leading me on. Marysyas is a delight, Leon.

LEON. Oh, yes, I suppose, yes. I mean, she's always been.

PETER. You are one lucky husband, Leon Nemenov. Yes. The luckiest, I would say…I've always had a crush on Marysyas…

LEON. Oh?

PETER. Yes.

LEON. Really? Now what do you find so alluring about Marysyas?

PETER. Oh, come on, Leon. Stop being so modest. Why, just this evening, I'm less and less watching the play and more and more my eyes dart up to your box to… to Marysyas. Watching her smile at some witty line or frown at a serious moment…

LEON. Is that so?

PETER. Yes.

LEON. I can't understand it. This is such a riveting play.

PETER. It doesn't matter. Marysyas just owns my eye.

LEON. Oh, Peter, you're really pouring it on, old friend – owns your eye. Come on…

PETER. I don't see it that way. You fellows marry and after a couple of years or so, a wife's beauty becomes fogged over by routine and familiarity…

LEON. Is that why you never married?

PETER. Not sure. But as I get older I regret it, Leon. At my age, a wife is someone I'd cherish now.

LEON. There are plenty of pretty girls in Saint Petersburg. Why this fixation on Marysyas?

PETER. Why? She is the perfect host whenever you have a party or a dinner at your home. She's...yes...She's graceful and intelligent and is in control of every man's attention. Every man looks on you with envy, Leon. You must love Marysyas with such ardor.

LEON. I?...Oh...Yes...I suppose...Yes...Yes...Marysyas...

(The lights blink.)

PETER. Well...Time for the second act, my friend.

LEON. Yes...See you again.

PETER. My best regards to Marysyas...

(**LEON** *crosses to* **MARYSYAS.**)

(to the audience) That night at home...well...listen for yourselves...

(**MARYSYAS** *comes to life.*)

LEON. At the intermission tonight, I ran into Peter Semyenich...

MARYSYAS. Oh, who was he with?

LEON. No one.

MARYSYAS. Didn't he used to escort what's-her-name...

LEON. Who can keep track of Peter Semyenich's comings and goings?

MARYSYAS. And you and he discussed real estate for the whole intermission?

LEON. On the contrary. We spent the whole time speaking only of you.

MARYSYAS. Of me?

LEON. Of you. Well, I should say he did. I couldn't get him off the subject of you.

MARYSYAS. What prompted that?

LEON. I don't know. But he couldn't stop glowing with admiration for you.

MARYSYAS. Peter Semyenich?

LEON. Yes...

MARYSYAS. I see...

LEON. Yes. Your beauty, it seems, owns his eye…he said…

MARYSYAS. Oh?

LEON. And he also complimented your grace and your intelligence…

MARYSYAS. Oh?

LEON. *(laughs)* What a character that man is.

MARYSYAS. He always seemed like a…a nice man…

LEON. I guess he's all right. But the way he went on about you, why, he had more puff than a French pastry.

MARYSYAS. Puff?…

LEON. Oh, God, yes. He told me that at our parties, every man there envies me…

(**LEON** *laughs.*)

MARYSYAS. He said so?

LEON. Oh, he poured it on, I'll say…

MARYSYAS. Perhaps he was trying to be nice…just giving you a compliment…

LEON. Marysyas, when we give a party all the women attending are ravishing, I can tell you.

MARYSYAS. Oh, yes…No…No question about that, Leon. All the women are…yes…all…

(**MARYSYAS** *and* **LEON** *freeze.*)

PETER. Next, I purposely run into Leon again where he buys cigars. After some perfunctory small talk about the weather and real estate…

(**LEON** *unfreezes and crosses to* **PETER.**)

I coil around his brain and squeeze a bit more… *(to* **LEON***)* You know, Leon. I sold a house in the country to a portrait painter…

LEON. You don't say…

PETER. Yes…It's near a stream and willow trees surround the house. This painter snared a commission from a prince – 2,000 rubles – he said, to paint the face of a beauty that – how did he put it – typifies the ideal beauty of Russian womanhood…

LEON. Two thousand rubles…

PETER. No sooner had this painter discharged the words from his mouth, Leon, I thought of your Marysyas…

LEON. My…

PETER. Yes…An artist won't find anyone more worthy of the title, Russian beauty, than she. But I knew it would be out of line for me to give your wife's name and your address on such a…well…on such a matter without permission…

LEON. I see…I'm sure this portrait painter will find some fair Russian damsel. Yes. This city is rife with them…

(**LEON** *crosses back to* **MARYSYAS,** *who unfreezes and looks at herself in a hand mirror.* **LEON** *buries his head in a newspaper.* **PETER** *adresses audience.*)

PETER. I know Leon. And I knew he'd run right home with this dollop of flattery. And by God, he did…Observe…

MARYSYAS. But do you, yourself, Leon, think I typify the ideal Russian woman? Leon?

LEON. I don't know about such things. You know that. I'm just repeating what Peter Semyenich said in the cigar store.

MARYSYAS. I didn't know Peter smoked cigars.

LEON. Maybe he started. I don't know. In my opinion I think the man has a case on you, he so overdoes the praise.

(**MARYSYAS** *looks in the hand mirror and smiles.*)

MARYSYAS. I suppose you're right, Leon.

LEON. What're you doing? It's time for dinner.

MARYSYAS. You go down and I'll be right along.

(**LEON** *goes off.* **MARYSYAS** *looks again in her hand mirror and smiles this way and that until she is satisfied that she typifies the ideal of a Russian woman. Then she freezes.*)

PETER. Oh, yes, the quest continues…

(**LEON** *walks on and crosses to* **MARYSYAS** *who unfreezes.*
LEON *examines her eyes.*)

MARYSYAS. Are you going to tell me what you're doing?
Leon?

LEON. That man's daft, I tell you, daft.

MARYSYAS. Who's daft?

LEON. Peter Semyenich. He tells me that one of your eyes
is darker than the other.

MARYSYAS. What?

LEON. Peter says that one of your eyes is darker than the
other and this gives you an exotic look.

MARYSYAS. Peter Semyenich said…

LEON. Yes. But I'll be damned if I see it. Daft…He's just
plain daft.

(**LEON** *crosses off.* **MARYSYAS** *picks up her hand mirror
and looks into her eyes.*)

MARYSYAS. Hmmm…Hmmm…It could be. This right eye
could be…maybe it is…That man looked so closely at
my eyes that he could detect this…Exotic…Hmmm…

(**MARYSYAS** *freezes.*)

PETER. Isn't she dazzling? Ah, my dearest Marysyas…but I
said this couldn't be rushed. What I'm doing is actually a precision realigning of brain cells. I would say
that I struck, oh, about a dozen times in the manner
I've demonstrated to you here.

(**LEON** *rushes on and* **MARYSYAS** *unfreezes.*)

LEON. Marysyas…Marysyas…

MARYSYAS. Leon?

LEON. I saw Peter Semyenich at a business meeting today…

MARYSYAS. Oh, Peter…Yes…How is he?

LEON. He apologizes to you and to me that he has missed
our gatherings for months now.

MARYSYAS. He's not ill, Leon, don't tell me that…

LEON. Not at all.

MARYSYAS. Thank God! I mean…I hope all of our friends are in good health.

LEON. He's fine. He's just been so busy, he tells me.

MARYSYAS. And when, when will I…will we see him again?

LEON. He said some time next year.

MARYSYAS. Next year? No…

LEON. What is it, Marysyas?

MARYSYAS. Nothing…Nothing at all…

LEON. You suddenly went pale…

MARYSYAS. No…No…I'm just…just curious about…about what Peter Semyenich is doing…with his life, I mean…

LEON. Some big land deal he's involved in…Dividing large tracts of land into smaller parcels…Working with surveyors and all that…You know what that oddball also said…

MARYSYAS. Tell me, tell me, tell me, Leon, tell me…

LEON. Are you ready for this?

MARYSYAS. My ears are curling into a cup, Leon.

LEON. Peter Semyenich says, explain to me, Leon. What? I answer. Tell me, he went on, why doesn't your Marysyas go on the stage…

MARYSYAS. The stage?…How I love the stage…

LEON. Her looks, he says, should be for the whole world to enjoy. People would pay, Leon, he said, to watch Marysyas…

MARYSYAS. Oh, my…Oh my God…

LEON. I knew you'd get a laugh out of this, too. So extraordinary is she, he says, that she must have royal lineage in her background somewhere.

MARYSYAS. Well…I…I had an uncle who was a sergeant in the Tsar's guard…

LEON. I hardly think that counts as a royal line. Your uncle had no means, so he joined the army.

MARYSYAS. True, but…well…What else did Peter have to say? Not that it means anything, but you always have such amusing stories about your encounters with him.

LEON. What else? Let's see...Oh, yes, how could I have forgotten this. God. Now you know how the man exaggerates...

MARYSYAS. No...I mean, yes...he does exaggerate...Yes... But tell me anyway...

LEON. Remember now, Marysyas, at this business meeting, we'd been drinking wine.

MARYSYAS. I understand...Wine...Yes...

LEON. After the meeting, when I was helping him get into a carriage, he rambled on that if he weren't a good Christian, he would fight a duel with me to have you...A duel...

(*He laughs and mimes shooting a pistol.*)

MARYSYAS. No...a duel?

LEON. (*laughing*) Can you believe it?

(**MARYSYAS** *feigns laughing with* **LEON.**)

He's so funny, Marysyas...Before his coach pulled away, he said... (*laughing again*) He said...He said...

MARYSYAS. (*laughing*) Stop laughing, Leon, and tell me what dear Peter said...

LEON. He said...He said...Are you ready?...He said...that if he were Turgenev, he would make you the stunning heroine of one of the great Russian novels...Can you imagine that?...Marysyas, a two volume set?

(**LEON** *laughs again.* **MARYSYAS** *does not laugh this time. She looks past* **LEON** *with far away eyes.*)

MARYSYAS. You were right, Leon, when you said I'd get a good laugh from this story...

LEON. Of course, I'm right. He exaggerates these qualities in you, because the poor clod has no wife of his own around all the time.

(**MARYSYAS** *and* **LEON** *freeze.*)

PETER. By this time, the wife is a boiling pot of desire. I religiously stay away from the next party, Marysyas' birthday celebration, even though on my printed invitation, Marysyas pens a personal note:

"Peter, it's been so long since I've seen you. Please try to attend." Please, she had underlined. I send my regrets with a large bouquet of roses. It's her birthday. Let her ruminate on age creeping up, time running out – you know how the mind plays on itself…Then the point comes to make the decisive move. Thus I make the key plant of information…

*(***LEON*** and **MARYSYAS** *unfreeze.)*

LEON. News…

MARYSYAS. What news?

LEON. Well, I'm riding home in a carriage and whom do you think I see sitting on a bench on Nevesky Boulevard – Peter Semyenich.

MARYSYAS. Oh, Leon…

LEON. What?

MARYSYAS. I said, Oh? Leon…So you stopped your cab and spoke, I hope. How is he?

LEON. Not well…

MARYSYAS. Not well? What did you say to him? Did he mention me? I mean to say, what nonsense is he spouting now?

LEON. Well, this time, there was no such nonsense, Marysyas.

MARYSYAS. No?…

LEON. No. To tell you the truth, no nonsense at all.

MARYSYAS. What has happened, Leon?

LEON. Peter Semyenich has become melancholy… morose…

MARYSYAS. Morose?…

LEON. Maybe beyond morose even. A more despondent man I can't remember knowing.

MARYSYAS. Oh, Peter…No…

LEON. I asked, what's the matter with you? Why do you sit on this bench with your head in your hands?

MARYSYAS. His poor head in his poor…

LEON. Yes…He poured his heart out to me.

MARYSYAS. He…He did?…

LEON. I am so alone, so cut off, he said. All I do is work and for what, Leon? For whom? For no one, Leon, I have no one. Each night, he said, I sit here on the bench at Nevesky Boulevard, near the fountain with these recurring thoughts of ending it all…That's what he's thinking.

MARYSYAS. Don't you dare, Peter…Leon, that…that poor man…

LEON. I know. I know. Don't be surprised if the fool does something to make us all cringe. He was that low in spirit, Marysyas…

MARYSYAS. I understand perfectly, Leon.

LEON. We must pray for him, Marysyas.

MARYSYAS. We shall, Leon.

LEON. I'm sorry to bring you such news…

MARYSYAS. You had no choice. He's my…Your close friend…

LEON. I'll go wash up for dinner now…Though that man has ruined my appetite…

(**LEON** *crosses off.*)

MARYSYAS. Leon goes to bed early…I'll…yes…I'll take a cab to the boulevard to the fountain…If someone sees me…I'll say…No…I don't care who sees me…I don't care…Peter needs me…I can feel it in every pore in my body…Peter…Oh, God…I feel as if I've let you down!

(**MARYSYAS** *runs off.* **PETER** *places a bench stage right center. He sits.*)

PETER. So I sit and wait and I know Marysyas' fate and my own. There's still a chill, but the evenings now are warm enough to enjoy the fresh air. A perfect night for the boa constrictor to swallow the rabbit. How do

I know my Marysyas shall be here? Why, it's all been planned that way. Hasn't it?

(Slowly **MARYSYAS** *enters. She wears a rabbit fur wrap. He looks at her. She sees him and stops, to a great fanfare of music.)*

MARYSYAS. Peter…

PETER. Marysyas…

(He rises.)

MARYSYAS. My darling…

PETER. You're here, woman of my dreams? Can it be? Am I hallucinating?

MARYSYAS. No…I'm here for you…

PETER. Oh, Marysyas…

MARYSYAS. Oh, Peter…

(They embrace. **PETER** *devours her with a kiss. They freeze. Lights slowly fade.)*

CHEKHOV. Don't be too quick to judge or cast the first stone. Some would argue that a passionate relationship with Peter is better than only a lifetime of apathy from Leon. Some would argue otherwise. As with all of these women, don't forget, we saw them in turn of the twentieth century Russia…Today, in your era, no men or women would think or behave as we've seen in these characters I've created. But it has been my pleasure to share their past and mine with you. With that, I bid you goodnight…

End

Also by
Jules Tasca…

Beginnings, Six One Act Plays

Four Way Split

The Grand Christmas History of the Andy Landy Clan

The Jew of Bologna

Princess Antigone

Sleep in Chains: Jekyll's Nightmare

Spells

Spirit of Hispania: Hispanic Tales

Telling Wilde Tales…

Will

OTHER TITLES AVAILABLE FROM BAKER'S PLAYS

FOUR WAY SPLIT

Jules Tasca

The Duty of Saints
1m, 2f

A Bishop requests a meeting - with a young woman journalist he has known since her childhood who has been writing critical articles about the Church - and her mother. He intends to discuss the beatification and potential canonizing of the girl's sister, a missionary nun killed abroad. During the meeting he discovers that the image he held of the family was an illusion, in which he unwittingly participated, as she reveals a dark family secret.

The Death of Bliss
1m, 1f

A young Palestinian man is honored by being chosen as a suicide bomber. An emotional crisis emerges when he discovers that his young wife is pregnant with their first child, and he must choose between honor and family.

Devil Dead Day
2m, 2f

Two devout sisters discover that a third sister has a hidden life, a sacrilege against God in their faith, and decide to help her "see Jesus" in the most extraordinary way.

The Beauty of Prayer
3m

When, after a successful operation to remove a brain tumor, his son drops out of Rabbinical college, a Rabbi blames the doctor for destroying the boy's future. The father discovers the true meaning of "life" in a painful revelatory discussion, and wounds are healed.

BAKERSPLAYS.COM

OTHER TITLES AVAILABLE FROM BAKER'S PLAYS

TELLING WILDE TALES...

Adapted for the Stage by Jules Tasca

Flexible Casting / Bare Stage

This full evening's entertainment includes *The Birthday of the Infanta,* a sad tale of the broken hearted hunchback brought to the palace of the Princess of Spain; *The Star Child,* a poignant portrait of a boy who thinks he was sent to earth by a shooting star; *The Happy Prince,* in which a statue and a bird, through their generosity and unselfish spirits, rekindle hope and understanding in their small city; *The Nightingale and the Rose,* the bittersweet story of love and self-denial; and *The Young King,* a tale full of hope for man's happiness when a young king discovers human compassion on the day of his coronation.

9 780874 403381